Jessica Harriet's New Neighbours

MICHAEL RATNETT and JUNE GOULDING

RED FOX

For the monsters who live in our street

A Red Fox Book

Published by Random House Children's Books
20 Vauxhall Bridge Road, London SW1V 2SA
A division of The Random House Group Ltd
London Melbourne Sydney Auckland
Johannesburg and agencies throughout the world

1 3 5 7 9 10 8 6 4 2

First published in Great Britain by Hutchinson Children's Books 1994
Red Fox edition 1999

Printed in Singapore

RANDOM HOUSE UK Limited Reg. No. 954009

ISBN 0 09 187305 3

'Hooray!' said Jessica Harriet. 'Today's the day our new neighbours move in. I wonder what they'll be like.'
    But her favourite toy, the Slurpglurpgobblebeast, just smiled.

Jessica Harriet and the Slurpglurpgobblebeast went straight to the window to keep watch.

It was a very busy morning. And they didn't have to wait long before some very FURRY characters came by.

'Goodness,' said Jessica Harriet. 'I hope they're our new neighbours. They could take us on picnics and invite us round for toast and honey.'

But the BEARS marched straight past. STOMP! STOMP! STOMP!
    They were not Jessica Harriet's new neighbours.

'Oh dear,' said Jessica Harriet.
   But the Slurpglurpgobblebeast said nothing.
   So Jessica Harriet and the Slurpglurpgobblebeast sat
and waited again.

Soon they heard a noise above them. As they looked up
some very MAGICAL people flew by.

'Wowee!' said Jessica Harriet. 'I hope they're our new neighbours. They could teach me spells, and I could change all my friends into slimy frogs and lumpy toads!'

'Good morning,' said the GIANT.

'Phew!' said Jessica Harriet. 'I'd love you to be our new neighbour. You could lift us up at night to see the stars, and we could make dens in your boots!'

But the GIANT just laughed, and shook his head.

And then he strode away over the houses. THUD! THUD! THUD! He was not Jessica Harriet's new neighbour.

'Hummph!' said Jessica Harriet.
   But the Slurpglurpgobblebeast said nothing.
   So Jessica Harriet and the Slurpglurpgobblebeast sat and watched again.

Soon some very FIERY characters came by.

'Gosh!' said Jessica Harriet. 'They've just *got* to be our new neighbours. They could take us on wonderful flights to far-off places and teach us how to breathe fire!'

But the DRAGONS had places of their own to go to. And they flapped right on past, snorting smoke and flames. WHOOSH!!!

They were not Jessica Harriet's new neighbours.

'Oh no,' said Jessica Harriet. 'It's not fair!'
    But the Slurpglurpgobblebeast said nothing.
    And so Jessica Harriet and the Slurpglurpgobblebeast
sat and waited one more time.

And then the most AMAZING characters of all came by!

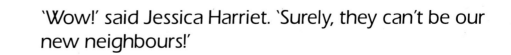

'Wow!' said Jessica Harriet. 'Surely, they can't be our new neighbours!'

But the family walked straight up to the front door of the empty house, and let themselves in.
They *were* Jessica Harriet's new neighbours!

'Hooray, hooray, hooray!' shouted Jessica Harriet. 'Our new neighbours are the best neighbours ever!'
    And the Slurpglurpgobblebeast grinned and grinned and grinned.

Then they rushed downstairs to tell everyone the news.

'Guess what?' said Jessica Harriet, bursting through the door. 'Our new neighbours are here, and they're PEOPLE. Real live people!'

'Really? Real live people?' said Dad. 'We'd better go and say hello.'
   'We'll go right away,' said Mum.

'Welcome to our street,' said Jessica Harriet's mum and dad.
'Thank you,' said the people. 'We're very pleased to be here.'
'Hello,' said Jessica Harriet to the new girl. 'My name's Jessica
Harriet and this is my best toy, the Slurpglurpgobblebeast.'

'Hello,' said the little girl. 'My name's Sarah, and this is *my* best toy, Snagglewort.'
    And they were friends at once.

'I'm glad you're my new neighbour,' said Jessica Harriet. 'I've always wanted to meet some people.'

'I'm glad too,' said Sarah. 'I've always liked monsters.'

And the Slurpglurpgobblebeast and Snagglewort just smiled.